A Christmas Anthology

A collection of Christmas stories
by Sheila Deeth

Contents

*One year I couldn't decide what to give my mother for Christmas
so I gave her a story. The next year I gave her another... and the next...
Then we had kids and Christmases became a little busy. Still...
fantasy, fable, faraway history, touches of faith, and more...
Mum kept the stories and now she says
I'm welcome to share them with you. Thanks, Mum!*

The Littlest Reindeer

Tam was the littlest reindeer in the herd. Born at the end of spring he had no idea what winter meant. Ice startled him. His thick coat warmed him. And snowflakes tasted like magic on his tongue.

Tam and his friends raced through the powder, tossing snow like mist behind their heels. Clean white fields churned into rolling lumps, and Tam was happy. But then he got hungry and realized all the grass was buried deep. His mother told him to dig with his nose, but ice crystals tickled his nostrils and made him sneeze. Then the snow crusted his eyes and made them hurt.

One winter's night, Tam woke in the dark and found the herd preparing for a long journey. Everyone stood with heads bent to the ground, making snuffling sounds as they pawed and ate the grass. Tam's mother said she'd been trying to wake him for ages.

"Why? Where are we going?"

But she wouldn't say. Tam thought he'd rather just sleep and not go anywhere, but didn't want to be left behind on his own. So he chomped some grass, sneezed a bit, and stepped into line. Soon the reindeer were gliding through trees, making hardly a sound, stepping softly on carpets of snow.

"Is it time?" a rabbit asked a hare. "The deer are running."

"Let's follow them."

The forest rustled with tiny whispers of noise, paws padding through shadows while snowflakes drifted. And the deer marched on.

Tam sulked at the very back of the herd and thought how much he wished he were still asleep. Soon he was drifting far behind and had to run to catch up. He skipped over rocks and bounded high in the air over broken tree-roots, which was really quite fun. Then he jumped over a long black log and found he'd gone over a cliff.

Tam landed on a slippery slope of snow and couldn't stay still. He stuck his legs out sideways to slow himself down. Then he lay on his stomach in a snowdrift and tried to catch his breath. A teardrop trickled down his nose and froze till he sneezed it away, then another one formed.

"Stop sniveling," said a voice somewhere above Tam's head.

Tam looked up into the rustling branches of a tree. *Was the tree talking?* His mother had told him never to speak to strangers, and a talking tree was definitely strange. But he thought he'd better at least apologize. "I'm sorry," said Tam. "I didn't mean to disturb you. I promise I'll stop crying."

He tried to slide away from the tree, but he couldn't see where he was going. The cliff rose up like a wall into the sky, snow fell like a blanket, and trees all around made the snow-covered ground invisible. So he stayed where he was.

Suddenly Tam heard a snuffling at his feet and saw a rabbit.

"Hello, Rabbit," said Tam. "What are you doing?"

"I'm waiting for my family."

Tam watched a whole herd of rabbits march out from the trees. They carried twigs on their shoulders, and each twig had a bag of food tied to its end, all wrapped in leaves. Squirrels scampered up as well, with strings of nuts tied around their necks.

"Where's everyone going?" Tam asked.

"We're following the deer."

Oh good, thought Tam. Perhaps if he followed the rabbits and squirrels, he'd find his herd again. He started to skip and jump till he realized he might step on the smaller animals. "I'm sorry. Sorry. So sorry…"

A rabbit sucked its wounded paw and said, "That's quite all right. But do get going. I'm cold."

"How can I get going?" asked Tam. "I was going to follow you."

"No, silly," said the rabbit. "You're a deer. You have to lead."

Tam almost started to cry again but remembered his promise to the tree. Instead he sat in the snow and groaned. "I can't lead anyone. I don't know the way." The other animals all cried then instead.

An owl swooped overhead and landed in the tree, which shook its branches angrily, sending owl and snowflakes tumbling to the ground. "Tu whoo," said the owl.

"Hello," said Tam. "Aren't you an owl?"

"Yes of course I'm an owl. Who else would say 'Tu whoo'?"

"I don't know," said Tam.

"Well, of course you don't. You're just a silly little deer."

The owl seemed rather snooty, and Tam didn't like it very much, but his mother always said owls are wise, so he asked for help anyway.

"I don't know where the deer go," said the owl. "That's their secret. I just follow them." The owl flew up onto Tam's shoulder and added, "Sometimes I ride with them."

"Well, you can't follow me," said Tam. "I don't know where I'm going. But if you fly up and see the deer, maybe you could lead us to them."

"I don't think so," said the owl. "It's snowing. If I fly up high, I won't see anything, and you won't see me."

Tam started to cry.

"You again," said the tree, throwing snowballs at Tam's nose.

"I'm sorry," said Tam. "I'm just so miserable."

"Well, go and be miserable somewhere else. I'm trying to rest."

One of the baby squirrels squeaked bravely. "But Mr. Tree, aren't you following the deer?"

"Certainly not! As if I'd go gallivanting around the countryside at my age!"

Tam tried to imagine a tree running around and almost laughed—*what would it use for feet?* Then he asked, "Can you really walk if you want to?"

"Of course."

"Can you see where you're going?"

"There'd be no point walking if I couldn't."

"And you're very tall." Tam paused, his nose glowing slightly as an idea formed in his mind. "Please," he said to the tree. "Please can you look where the deer have gone and tell us how to find them?"

"Will you go away if I tell you?"

"Yes. I promise."

"Like you promised not to cry?"

"No. Better than that."

"Well, they went thataway."

Tam looked around. "Which way?"

"Thataway."

"But which way is that?" Poor Tam couldn't see which way the tree was pointing, and neither could anyone else. "Please, Mr. Tree, you've got so many branches I don't know which ones are your hands. I'll never find my herd"

Now all the animals were crying again. Their snuffling and whimpering and wailing made the tree shake so angrily it pulled its roots right out the ground till they were stamping in snow. The feel of loose earth around its roots made the old tree feel young again, so it hummed a merry tune and danced a waltz. The animals stared, amazed.

"Please," said Tam, rather nervously, when the tree stopped dancing.

"Yes," said the tree, leaning down, dripping snow on his nose.

"Please, now you're walking anyway, could you show us the way to the deer?"

"Oh, very well." The old tree groaned. "But afterward you must promise never to annoy me ever again."

"We promise," all the animals said.

They made a very strange procession. The old tree creaked in the lead, and Tam hurried next to it with the owl on his back. Smaller animals sat in the roots of the tree. Beavers and badgers scurried behind. Swallows and starlings swooped among the branches. Soon the whole forest seemed to move as younger trees lifted their feet, or perhaps their roots, to join in.

They crossed over fields of snow, rivers of ice, and deserts of drifting sand. They climbed mountains and battled winds and gales. They swam through deep-flowing seas. And everywhere they went, more animals rushed to join them.

At last they came to a cold bright place where a star turned midnight into day. Sheep grazed on the hills, and Tam called out, "Have you seen a herd of deer going this way?"

"Yes," said the sheep. They pointed with their noses and everyone followed. Just over the next hill they found the deer gathered around the entrance to a stable. The owl flew up into the tree for a better view, while Tam rushed to his mother. He nuzzled her side to say sorry for getting lost, and she licked his nose. Then they both stared into the cave where a baby lay surrounded by shepherds with lambs and rich men with camels.

"Who are they all?" asked Tam.

"I don't know," said his mother. "But I know the baby's a king and all these people are giving him presents."

When the shepherds and kings had all gone away, the animals and trees made their way into the stable. Birds dropped feathers to make soft pillows. Rabbits and squirrels gave tufts of fur for a blanket. Even the trees made carpets of leaves on the floor.

Last of all, the reindeer marched in. Their leader had antlers reaching to the sky and a nose as red as sunshine on a clear day. He bent his head low over the baby. "I'm here," he said. "I've brought my herd. We're ready to keep our promise." Then the baby's messenger fastened a sleigh to all the reindeer and they started to fly, over seasons and settlements and countries and years, through peace-time and war-time and happiness and tears, bringing gifts to all ages and times for the baby's birthday.

"But we didn't give him a gift," said Tam as they flew.

"Yes, we did," said his mother. "Keeping the promise is our gift."

A Present for Sammy

Sammy was quite an ordinary dog—just a brown and white mongrel with wavy hair and tail and floppy ears. He lived in an ordinary house with an ordinary family—Mom and Dad, Pete and Carol and the baby. And he didn't know about winter because he was less than one year old.

It started to snow on Sammy's first Christmas Eve. It looked as though the sky was falling, and maybe someone had thrown a white carpet on top of the ground to protect it. Perhaps the carpet was meant to hold the world together while the sky fell apart. Oddly enough, no-one seemed to mind when Pete and Carol went out to play in the oddly broken world, so Sammy stood on the doorstep wondering what to do. He stepped one paw nervously onto the white, and it was cold! He wished he wore boots.

Sammy jumped up and down to keep warm, and snow flew all around him; fluffy white bits fluttered everywhere. Meanwhile the children made white balls which they threw for him to chase, but he could never find them. Then the mother told everyone to come in. A nice smell of dinner drifted out from the kitchen, and Sammy felt hungry. His coat steamed, and the white stuff melted to puddles around his dish while he fed.

After he'd eaten, Sammy went into the dining-room to join the family. They were still sitting at the table eating their dinners, of course, but when they finished the father went out into the hall. Meanwhile the children talked excitedly about something called Christmas that was going to happen tomorrow. Sammy heard the father climb upstairs. Then he heard him huffing and puffing and banging something around. Sammy went to the door, but no-one would let him out.

The father came back, covered in dust and cobwebs from the attic and carrying bright-colored boxes and sacks. Sammy barked, and everyone laughed. They all gathered in the living-room and sat around a big tree that stood in the corner. The mother and father had brought the tree home in the car a few days earlier. Sammy didn't know why they'd put a tree inside the house, but he wasn't allowed to water it or play with its leaves.

The children tugged bright strips of shiny paper out of the sacks and hung them on the tree. The mother and father took shiny round balls from the box and hung them up too. Soon the green, winter-tree looked like a bouquet of flowers. The mother and father even put flower-shaped lights on it and made them shine. Sammy still wasn't sure if he liked the tree or not, but he liked the lights because they felt warm.

Now it was it was time for the children to go to bed. Sammy barked and chased them upstairs; it was his job to make sure they did as they were told, and tonight... Well, tonight poor Sammy didn't understand why the children kept creeping down the stairs again and whispering and laughing. He understood even less why their parents didn't seem to be annoyed. The lights still shone on the tree. The dinner-plates were all washed and put away. The sky outside the window was still dark, and there was still that odd white stuff on the ground. Sammy lay down in his basket in the kitchen and hoped maybe tomorrow would be less strange.

Sammy had just managed to close his eyes when he heard the whole family walk into the kitchen—in the middle of the night! He tried to ignore them and pretended to be asleep, but he kept one eye half-open so he could see what they were doing. The mother filled the kettle with water and put it on the stove. The children got out a cup and saucer and plate which they put on a clean napkin on a shelf. Then the mother put a tea-bag next to the cup, and some milk in a jug and some sugar in a bowl. Finally, she opened a tin of spicy pastries and put one on the plate. It was all Sammy could do to avoid licking his lips. The pastry smelled so nice.

When they'd finished laying these things out, they all went away again and closed the kitchen door. The children raced upstairs, and the lamp-shade in the kitchen rattled as they slammed the doors to their rooms. In a few minutes, the parents went up more slowly to say goodnight, and everything went quiet.

When he was sure no-one was coming back to the kitchen, Sammy crept over to the shelf where the pastry was. He tried to jump up, but the shelf was too high. Then he looked for something he might climb on, but there was nothing nearby. After a while he gave up and went back to his basket. He felt sure he would never fall asleep though, with such a tantalizing smell in the air.

Later, when Sammy was almost asleep, he heard the father open the kitchen door. "Good night, Sammy," he said quietly. Sammy wagged his tail a bit to show he'd heard. Then the father closed the door and went away.

This time Sammy really did fall asleep. When he awoke, it was still dark, and the moon was shining through the window. He thought how glad he was that he wasn't the sort of dog that has to howl at the moon. Then he heard a noise and saw the kitchen door start to open, very slowly. At first, he thought it must be one of the family, but instead a total stranger in a bright red suit walked in. He was a heavily-built man with a large waist, a long white beard, and a smiling face. Sammy wasn't sure if he should frighten the man away or welcome him, so he just sat back and looked at him instead.

The stranger lit the gas under the kettle then waited for the water to boil. When it boiled, he used the tea-bag to make some tea and put sugar and milk into it. Then he picked up the cup in one hand and the pastry in the other and started to eat and drink. Sammy wagged his tail and looked up hopefully. The man saw him and put down his cup while he broke the pastry in two. Sammy raced forward to pick up the crumbs but found, instead, that the man was offering a whole half a pastry, all for Sammy. The happy dog simply couldn't believe his luck! Whoever this stranger was, he was very, very nice.

When the stranger had finished his tea, he went into the room with the tree. He left the door of the kitchen open, so Sammy followed him. The lights were still shining on green branches like magical flowers, and there was a huge sack lying in the middle of the floor. Sammy crept forward to sniff at the sack, but the stranger held him back. Then the stranger reached in and began to remove lots of parcels, one by one. The parcels were covered in bright-colored paper decorated with pictures, but Sammy couldn't quite see what the pictures were, and the man wouldn't let him take a closer look. Each parcel seemed to have a label on it.

The man read the labels and put the parcels in five piles at the bottom of the tree. But his sack didn't seem to get any emptier. It stayed huge and wide and lumpy in the middle of the floor.

Eventually the stranger sat back on his heels and looked at Sammy. "Your turn now," he said, holding one final parcel in front of Sammy's nose. This one was covered in blue paper with pictures of a white-bearded man wearing a red suit. It smelled of something really nice. Sammy took the parcel carefully between his teeth. Then he tried to tear the paper off. It was held with some thick sticky stuff, but after a while Sammy managed to bite enough holes so he could get in.

Inside the parcel, Sammy found a new plastic bone that looked like, and smelled like, and even tasted like the real thing! He wagged his tail delightedly and licked the stranger's hand. Then he curled up on the rug, surrounded by scraps of bright blue paper and sticky-tape, and he started to chew. After a while he fell asleep again and never saw the stranger climb into the chimney and disappear.

Early next morning, the children were running around noisily upstairs, but Sammy stayed asleep. The parents got up, and everyone got dressed, then the family came downstairs all together. The father opened the door to the living-room, and everyone raced in.

"Daddy, look!" said Pete as he stopped in the middle of the room. There was Sammy, fast asleep on the rug in the middle of a mountain of blue Christmas wrapping paper, with a plastic bone between his paws.

Sammy woke up at the noise and opened his eyes. It was only his family—nothing to worry about—so he bent his head over the bone and started to chew again as if nothing was wrong.

The parents gazed at Sammy in amazement. "I'm sure I shut him in the kitchen," said the father.

"And the door to the living-room was closed—I only just opened it," said the mother.

"How on earth did Sammy get in here?"

"And how on earth did he find his own present amongst all the others?"

No-one could solve the mystery. How could a dog walk through two closed doors and read all the labels on the presents and find the one with "Sammy" written on it? How could a dog open a parcel all on his own? And why were there crumbs of mince pie all around his whiskers, when he couldn't possibly have climbed high enough to reach Santa's food on the shelf?

"It must be magic," said Carol.

"It must have been Santa," said Pete.

Then Cathy, the baby, crawled to where all the presents still waited under the tree. Soon there was wrapping paper of every possible color strewn across the floor, and Sammy had to find somewhere else to chew his bone in peace.

A Shortage of Chimneys

We made Christmas cards in school today. I made one with a picture of Santa and his sleigh and his reindeer landing on a chimney. There was smoke coming out of the chimney. I made the smoke out of cotton wool, and I made Santa's bear out of cotton wool too. But I colored the rest of the picture with crayons.

Someone asked the teacher why Santa doesn't get burned when he goes down all those chimneys. She said it was magic, but everyone knows he's got a fireproof suit really. Someone else asked how the reindeer fly without wings. I think they grow invisible wings just for Christmas. I drew them on my card, but only faintly because they're invisible.

We always make Christmas cards in the last week of school. Last year we did pictures of Jesus, Mary, and Joseph in the stable. Pete Howarth swiped my red crayon 'cause he said the baby Jesus had to have a red halo, then he wouldn't give it back. I wanted to draw a Santa in the stable, but I couldn't without my red crayon.

I wish I knew why Santa always wears red. Cathy Collins says it's so that you can't see him when he comes down a chimney 'cause fires are red too. But nobody sees Santa come down chimneys anyway 'cause they're all asleep. Cathy says her brother saw Santa once, but I don't believe her. I nearly saw him last Christmas, I think... I think I even talked to him. But everybody says it was only a dream, so it can't have been true...

Anyway, Santa can't come down a chimney in our house 'cause we haven't got a chimney. So what will he do?

***

Santa wasn't too happy when central heating became popular. Lots and lots of houses were built without chimneys, and he always used to come down people's chimneys at Christmas. Of course, he *is* Santa, so he could always get in some other way, but none of them felt right. One year he used a special key that let him unlock everyone's front door, but he had a lot of trouble with dogs who thought it was their job to bite his ankles. Then he tried climbing through downstairs' windows and nearly got caught by a policeman who thought he was a burglar. Next, he tried magic—walking through walls or floating through the ceiling or the floor. But it wasn't anywhere near as much fun as huffing his way down a chimney with a toy-sack on his back.

One Christmas, Santa decided to park his sleigh in the air and float through people's windows. He had to use two spells, one to make the glass disappear in the window and one to make himself float. Of course, he used another magic spell afterward to put the glass back.

Santa had gone through lots of windows this way when he came to Michael's room, and he'd not had any problems. It wasn't as good as climbing down chimneys, but he was quite enjoying himself. The trouble was, none of the houses he'd been to so far had double-glazing, and Michael's house had. When Santa cast his spell to make the glass disappear, he only made one pane of glass disappear. Then he tried to float through the window and banged straight into the second pane of glass with his nose.

The reindeer thought this was very funny and jumped around with laughter. All the bells jangled brightly in their harnesses, and this woke Michael up.

Of course, Santa realized straight away what was wrong and said his magic spell again. He floated peacefully into the room, but it was already too late. Michael was well and truly awake and couldn't possibly be convinced that he was just dreaming. "Hello, Santa!" he shouted happily.

Santa turned around to look at him. "Shush, Michael," he said. "You don't want to wake your sister do you?"

"Why not?" asked Michael.

"Because your mom would be annoyed," said Santa—he was very wise about these things. So Michael stopped talking.

Santa put his sack on the floor and started loading presents into the stocking on the end of Michael's bed. It wasn't a real stocking of course. You could fit most of Michael into this stocking, besides both his feet. But this was a Christmas stocking, meant to hold presents, not legs. It had a picture of Santa on one side, and it was big and red and fluffy. Even so, it couldn't hold all of Michael's presents, so Santa had to put some parcels on the floor next to it. Michael began to crawl out of bed to get a better look at them, but then he saw Santa watching and crept back again.

"I always wondered how you got into houses without chimneys," Michael whispered, when Santa had finished his job.

"Really," said Santa, sitting down on the edge of the bed. "How did you think I did it?"

"I don't know," said Michael. "But you did look funny when you banged your nose on my window."

"You didn't see me bang my nose," said Santa. "You were asleep."

"Yes, but I saw you just afterward when I woke up, and the reindeer were still laughing."

Oh dear, thought Santa. If he was going to bang his nose and look funny, maybe this wasn't such a good way to get into houses. He wished he could think of something better. Then he thought of asking Michael if *he* could think of a good way to do it. After all, Michael *lived* in a house.

"If you can think of a really good way," said Santa, "I'll give you a really special present."

"What present?" Michael asked.

"A dream."

Santa went out then to give Michael's sister and his Mom and Dad their presents. Meanwhile Michael sat up in bed trying to think of something wonderful because, after all, a dream from Santa was bound to be very, very nice. Michael frowned and frowned and thought and thought, and the reindeer outside his window began to get restless. Michael watched them toss their heads and stamp and paw at the air. They looked just like their pictures on Christmas cards. Then Michael had an idea.

He crept to the end of his bed again to look carefully at his Christmas stocking. He wasn't looking at the presents now—he knew he mustn't do that until tomorrow. But he looked at the picture of Santa on the side of the stocking, to see if it really looked like him. Most especially, he looked to see if the Santa in the picture had a really big sack. Then he crawled back under the bedclothes and smiled as he thought of his wonderful idea.

Santa came back in a few minutes. His sack was empty, and he tossed it through the window back onto the sleigh. Michael watched as it magically filled up again. Then Santa sat beside him.

"Well, young man. Have you thought of anything?"

"Yes," said Michael happily.

"What is it then?" asked Santa. So Michael began.

At Christmas, everyone gets Christmas cards and Christmas decorations, and they put up stockings with pictures of Santa on them. They even hang toy Santas on trees and pictures of Santa in their windows. Every house, or at least nearly every house, has a picture or a toy Santa somewhere inside. All the real Santa would have to do to get into a house would be to magic himself into his picture and then climb out.

Santa thought about this for a minute then climbed off the bed to look at Michael's stocking. "Do you mean like this?" he asked... and vanished.

Michael gasped and sat up straight, looking around. Then he saw his stocking begin to wobble and suddenly the picture on the side came to life and stood up, a real live Santa. There was a big white patch left on the stocking where the picture had been.

"Yes," said Michael. "Just like that."

Then Santa magicked the picture back into the stocking and sat down on Michael's bed again.

"Do you like my idea?" Michael asked.

"Yes," said Santa, huffing and puffing a bit. "It was rather fun, I thought. Much more fun that walking through walls or floating in through windows."

"And bumping your nose?"

Santa rubbed his nose and laughed. "Yes, definitely more fun than bumping my nose. But now I must be going," he added, as the reindeer shook their heads at him. "So, it's time for your special present. There's only one thing though," Santa added, looking down as Michael's eyes began to droop

"What?" asked Michael.

"Well, I'm not allowed to let anyone remember that they've seen me, so now you're going to have to forget all about everything that's happened tonight."

"But how can I forget?"

"I'll put a spell on you," said Santa. "It will make all this"—he waved his arms around the room—"seem like a dream. And, of course, everyone always forgets their dreams."

"But what about my present?" asked Michael. "What about my special dream?"

"That's our little secret," said Santa, smiling. "You see, you *won't* forget the dream. Every Christmas you'll dream it again and you'll know you really did see me and talk to me. In all the whole wide world, you'll be the only one who remembers."

***

So you see, I really did see Santa, and I really talked with him. But I'll wake up in a minute, and then it will seem like a dream again.

The Star

It wasn't a very important star. It gave its light neither to people nor to planets. Alone in its dark corner of the universe it shone and waited, and then, at its appointed time, it died.

The light from the death of the star began its journey across the heavens. It shone like a sun in the night-time sky of a planet called earth. And the people of earth followed the star as a sign from God. Because the star died—because it died when it did—they called it the star of Bethlehem. And through all the years that followed, they remembered its light.

No-one was sure who first saw the star. There were travelers on the roads of Judea who thought its light must be God's curse on the Romans. There were shepherds who struggled to calm their sheep, made nervous by the unaccustomed day. And there were wise men in the East who consulted their prophecies, wondering what great events were about to happen. All these people followed the star, each in their own way, and none of them really knew what the bright star meant.

The streets of Bethlehem were crowded. People had come from all over the country to be registered in the Roman census. The inns were filled with soldiers and guests. Private homes overflowed with long-forgotten relatives. And the streets were packed, as beggar and rich man laid out their cloaks together in search of rest.

Pilgrims continued to pour along the road. They carried elderly parents and young children in carts or rode on donkeys. There was even an occasional camel. Ahead of them, the dusty trail offered no hope of rest—just more crowds, more sleepless nights, and more bureaucracy.

At the city gates, an old woman stood waiting. She took charge of the donkeys and camels, as people arrived, and led them off to the stables for shelter and food. There was room in the stables, though there was no room in the town.

Roman guards stood watching the pilgrims, watching as the crowds passed silently through the gates to mingle with the noisier throngs within.

***

In the East, wise men were looking at the new star and wondering what it meant. Each left the observatory to consult their books, studying positions and angles and prophecies until an answer could be found. A few nights later they met again. "What did you find?" they asked each other.

"I found that a great king is born," said one.

"I read that a new god has entered the world," said another.

"I found life and death," said a third, "and they were both the same."

Then they asked each other what they should do and decided to follow the star, to find the king or god and do him homage. So they loaded their camels with gifts and food, and set off into the desert.

***

The sheep were restless. It was time to move to new pastures. Shepherds complained at all the work that would mean.

Meanwhile, a young couple arrived at the gates of Bethlehem—a man leading a donkey with a woman riding on it. They handed the donkey's reins to the woman at the gate and paid her for her services. Then they entered. Joseph smiled at his wife.

"I think the donkey will get more shelter than us," he said.

Mary smiled back, saying nothing.

In the city they joined with the thronging crowds and began to knock on doors to find a place to stay. The answer was the same as they'd heard along the way—there was no room. Poor Mary was close to giving birth, and Joseph grew afraid for her and the child. What chance would they have if she had to lie in the street for the baby to be born?

As they left each house, Mary walked more slowly, seeming more and more tired, her smiles more weary and dejected. At last Joseph saw she could go no further, so they sat down together, leaning on a wall.

"Will it be soon?" Joseph asked.

"Tonight," said Mary.

Sun set and the city gates were closed. The bolts clanged home, and a heavy silence descended with the darkness. Light streamed from the windows of inns. Sounds of Roman revelry and smells of sweaty soldiers filled the air.

Houses were lit up too, humming with the noise of too many people crowded in tiny rooms. But in the streets all was quiet. Children clung to their mothers and slept. Fathers kept watch till sleep claimed them too. And beggars crept, seeking what meager pickings they could find.

***

The wise men stopped at a green oasis and looked up at the star.

"Is it growing brighter?" one asked.

"It seems so."

"We must be near."

***

As night fell the shepherds lit their fires and laid plans for the watch. Wives and children settled into the huts they'd built on the hillside. And the sheep began to rest. This hill was closer to Bethlehem than they liked to be—from the top you could even see the town—but they stayed hidden behind an outcrop, where the winds were less wild.

Stars came out in the cloudless sky. The new star seemed brighter still, casting shadows far from the fire. The sheep murmured, disturbed by its strangeness. And the shepherds talked in the firelight while their families slept.

In the city, the woman returned from the stables through a back entrance behind the inn. She was worried and still unready for sleep. In her mind she kept thinking of the couple she'd seen late in the afternoon—a man who had laughed with his wife about how well the animals would fare. His wife had seemed so close to bearing her child.

The woman knew she'd never rest until she knew the young couple had found shelter. She asked her husband if he'd seen them.

"I've seen a thousand people today," he answered, annoyed. "D'you expect me to remember one man and one woman?"

"I remember them," said his wife.

"Yes, well, you're a woman."

So she left the inn quietly and began to wander the streets. There were people everywhere, asleep or close to sleep, or wakeful beggars following till she shooed them away. Then she found the couple she was looking for.

Mary lay against her husband's arm. Her face was tired and drawn, star-light reflecting from lines of sweat on her cheeks, dust from the streets and faint smudges of tears on her chin. Her eyes were closed, but her hands clenched and unclenched by her side, and she did not sleep.

Joseph looked up when he heard the woman's footsteps. He smiled sadly and held his wife more closely. Then the woman knelt beside him and spoke to him.

"She needs shelter," she said, looking at Mary.

"I know."

"I can take you to the stables," the woman offered. "It's all I have."

Joseph's eyes lit up at the thought. Suddenly he recognized the woman from the gate—the one who'd taken his donkey—and he trusted her.

"Thank you," he said. "You're very kind."

***

The wise men pitched their tents on the borders of Judea. In a Bethlehem stable, a baby started to cry. And the star shone bright.

The shepherds were talking, swapping tales by the fire, when suddenly the brightness of a million stars filled the air around them. They dove to the ground and covered their eyes in fear. A strong wind seemed to blow overhead, and the sheep bleated in distress. But the shepherds could not move.

Then a voice spoke from the space above their fire. "Fear not. I bring you tidings of great joy."

The shepherds looked up. The smoke had been replaced with the forms of men, bright beyond all brightness they'd ever known. Even the strange night star was eclipsed by this fiercely glorious intensity. But the strange bright men wore welcoming smiles and drove the shepherds' fear away with their gaze.

They had much to tell, these strangers in the sky. They talked of prophecies and redemption, of a child who was meant to be savior of all, born in a stable with animals and straw. And they charged the shepherds to go and pay homage to the boy.

***

It seemed the star truly burned brighter now. People began to wake in the city, curious at the lightness of the sky. The old woman awoke in her inn and looked out over starlit streets. Suddenly she knew. What other sign could this be? The baby was born!

Before she left, the woman packed a parcel for the mother and child; fresh broth in a pot, woolen cloths to keep them warm; even some milk in a jug. Then she stepped out toward the wall, to the small gate that led down the hill and on to the stables.

It seemed as if the star shone directly above the stable. Its light shafted through a high-cut window and lit on the family seated around the manger. The child lay in its mother's arms, eyes open and watching, small face at rest. And the mother smiled, contented and at peace.

Suddenly there was a sound outside. Voices spoke and footsteps shuffled on hay. Sheep and goats began to wander among the donkeys. The old woman stared. Shepherds came from the hills outside the town, dressed in their woolen cloths and rags and carrying their crooked staffs. They had some curious tale to tell of how an angel had sent them on their way. The mother smiled in welcome and held out her child. They knelt at its feet.

***

The wise men entered Judea the next day. They knew they were close to their journey's end, and they sought the nearest king to find his child. But the king had no child, only grown-up sons, and he had no answers to their questions, only rumors, so they journeyed on.

The king's wise men consulted their holy books and studied the star which seemed to shine brighter each night. At last they found a prophecy about a place called Bethlehem. "That's where a new king will be born," they said, and the old king was afraid.

***

The census was nearly over. Soon all these people would return to their homes. Mary and Joseph would leave the stable and take their son to Nazareth. And the old woman would return to keeping her inn in peace.

Then the strangers arrived, rich men in glorious clothes, with camels carrying their possessions. They stopped outside the city gates and would not speak with the guards. They pitched their tents right there on the hill, waiting for night.

When the star came out, they left their tents to the keeping of their servants and followed the light. They found the stable, and the baby, and they offered their gifts.

"I bring gold," said the first man, "for a king."

"I bring incense for a god."

"I bring myrrh for death."

***

King Herod had hoped the strangers would return but they chose a different path. He made his wise men check the prophecies again, becoming more and more sure that Bethlehem was the place where a new king was born. Then he ordered his soldiers to kill all the little children in Bethlehem. "I am king of Judea—only I—not any low-born infant, no matter what the stars say. And king I'll stay."

He didn't know that angels were carrying messages that night. An angel spoke to Joseph in a dream, and he fled with Mary and the baby, and the donkey, before the soldiers arrived.

***

So now the star is gone, and only its memory remains. Its light still travels the universe, fainter and fainter as distance takes its toll. In some far place perhaps it's shining now. People we have never known might ask, "What can this mean?" For the star was never an important star, and this earth of ours is just a speck among all the whirling dust of the universe. Judea was just a minor nation among those conquered by Rome. And yet, in the eyes of God, these things were the most important of all.

Following Sheep

In fields on the hills, sheep were sleeping. A few might wake and yawn or stretch. A few might wander, a lamb to its mother or mother to her lamb. A few might hear a distant sound and stir with gentle fear till the shepherd came. The sounds were just the sounds of night, and the night was deep and dark.

Above, unclouded, there were stars. Below, men and sheep lay in the cold. Sheep and shepherds were wrapped in wool, but only the shepherds had fire.

Across the hills, the lights of town glimmered in the clear night air. Lamps flickered closer where shepherds or soldiers patrolled. The world slept unmoving, unmovable. Stars twinkled, sheep murmured, and a shepherd put yet another log on the fire.

They didn't notice anything at first. It might have been dawn as the sky grew pale, except the eastern horizon stayed black and the sun still slept. Then the sheep began to stray.

It started somewhere in the direction of town. A whisper began to run through the flocks. Heads raised. Legs kicked and bodies scrambled into motion like a stream undammed. The sheep followed each other, all following unled. In a moment they were gone.

Lights swayed and voices shouted as the shepherds saw what had happened. They raced to stop their wandering flocks, but there were none to stop. The sheep and their sounds and their smells had disappeared in the false dawn, faded like shadows.

The shepherds stood silent, afraid. It was not the light that frightened them. Light was light. But sheep were food and clothing and coinage for tax. They needed those sheep.

Then the brightness grew like day, and fear greater than their loss struck the shepherds to the ground. Each crouched and covered his eyes. A voice, too bright and clear for the ears of men, called out, "Fear not!"

Fear not? Slowly the shepherds raised their faces and saw the shining white robes of angels from scriptures, or from God.

They could not know why God had chosen them to hear the news. They were just shepherds, keepers of sheep. But now they heard strange tidings that would change the world. In David's town—not Jerusalem, but in Bethlehem, the one-horse town of the great King David's birth—a promise was coming into the world. The savior, the Christ long foretold, was born as a child, and they'd find him in a stable, wrapped in cloths and lying in a manger.

The shepherds sought him out. Like sheep, they followed the sheep who had strayed, led now by an angel choir to stable and child. They found the infant king, and their flocks, and peace.

One of the shepherds remembered a prophecy then—after all, he'd studied the scriptures well, before he lost house and home to Roman taxes and started herding sheep. He spoke the words from Isaiah about how we, like sheep, have gone astray. "But now we've been found," he said. "Our shepherd's here."

Only a baby, but more than a baby; this night the Christ was born.

Anglo-Saxon Dreaming

Somewhere hidden in mist and snow was his home; a candle burning; Mia and the child; and a fire in the hearth. Somewhere there was a glow of warmth, but not here.

White stillness deadened sound and feeling. Silence, never quite complete, broken by sounds, sharp and sudden, afraid to be heard… A bird? The wind stirred distantly, and marsh-grass, brittle-frozen, broke. Unseen life scrabbled for warmth, while water whispered under ice.

The man stood listening, still as the cold night's falling. He shifted his hold on the stick in his hand, then planted it firmly on the ground and moved on. Ice cracked and snow crunched underfoot. Stick and step. Step and stick again.

Ice-crystals grew in his beard, while hands and feet grew numb. The white became gray as he walked on. Night falling, sky turned black. What was there in life but silence and cold… and Mia hiding in the blind night waiting for him… and the child? What else was there but to walk or die like an animal lost in winter's frozen wastes?

The stick slipped and he fell. Walk slower. Walk faster. The sharp cold of water stung his skin, and his clothes turned to ice. So cold. So still.

Gray ghosts of trees reached out to him. Roots clasped their jaws around his ankles while branches clawed his face. He felt for the path ahead with frozen hands and couldn't feel anymore when they touched twigs or bark. The trees hemmed him in, and it was too cold to fight them.

Silent in the gray of mist he saw the shapes of strangers. Voices unheard, he sensed the stirring of air with their speaking. Hands pulled him awake and laid him by a fire.

He stirred and found food offered, smelled strange scents of animals and warmth. He ate. The men were strangers and spoke a foreign tongue, even the shapes of their voices strange to him. Their animals didn't belong to his fens. Their clothes were alien to his mist and gray.

He was lost and a stranger here, so he rode with the strangers through their strange land, dry and warm under the light of an alien star. He came with them to a city he didn't know, stopped at a cave that seemed to be a stable. The curious star shone bright as day in the black night sky. In its clear-etched shadows, a man and woman stood holding a child.

The strangers knelt and he knelt with them, knees aching on hard dry earth. He saw the child, and he saw God. Others fell to their faces, pressing their mouths in the dirt. Young and old, rich and poor, dark and fair, tall and short, the strong and the weak knelt together. Dark Saxon and fair Angle prayed in a tongue that neither knew, united in love.

He believed it, though he didn't know how; this child commanding their worship would die for them.

***

The hay grew brittle, bathed in ice, and snow fell past his face. His clothes like boards pressed stiff and damp against him, his thick beard frozen, his body numb. There was no stable, only a faint light breaking through the trees to lead him on. Mia stood in the doorway of his home, their small son lying, safe and warm in her arms. There was a fire and Christmas food prepared to welcome him.

But it was an aching warmth. The child of his dream, the Christmas child, had died, and died for him—he wondered, *how could he know that?* But he had seen its birth this night—all time and space and all mankind united there as one.

Star Bright

Twinkle twinkle little star,

How I wonder what you are,

Up above the world so high

Like a diamond in the sky...

***

She sighed. It seemed the poem was never ended, as if there were another pair of lines eternally forgotten. She wondered why she'd never noticed that as a child.

The song finished and Anna smiled up at her. "Play it again, Mommy?"

Her mother pushed the arm on the plastic toy and pressed the button. "Just one more time, Anna, then go to sleep."

"Yes Mommy. One more time."

It was their nightly ritual, this playing of old songs to make Anna sleep. The one about the star seemed to be her favorite, just as it had been her mother's once. The record-player was one her own mother had given her one Christmas long ago, still working now for the grandchild she'd never seen. It was a kind of link with the past perhaps, with a time that she always felt had surely been kinder.

Curfew. The lights went out and the siren sounded to tell them to close their shutters. She heard Alan fastening wooden boards outside on the balcony. Another nightly ritual. The record ended, and she switched the music off.

"Good night, Anna."

"Good night, Mommy."

The song still spun its magic in her head as she left the room. It would be Christmas soon. Alan was building a doll's house for Anna's present. Pieces were strewn about the floor, and the air was scented with paint for doors and window-frames. She stood and watched him for a while, then got her sewing out and the pattern for the dolls. She had made the mother and father already and was working on the children.

"How many children d'you think?"

Alan looked up, confused. "Children?"

"For the doll's house."

"I thought you meant for us."

They'd hoped so much for a second child, but the rules said only one per couple now, and only then if you passed all their tests and paid enough money to finance the child's education before it was born. If every couple had only one child, wouldn't the country run out of people soon? It didn't make sense. But there again, war didn't make much sense either, and the papers were full of reports of dying and death.

"Three or four do you think?" Alan suggested.

"Four," she replied.

The alarm clock clanged its bell at nine o'clock. Time to switch off the lights—they couldn't afford electricity for more. And now they could take the shutters down without lighting the neighborhood for the bombers to see. They stood together on the balcony, listening to the quiet of the night. The sky was clear, stars shining down on them, and she thought of the song. Stars had been safe when she was a child, specks of sunshine in the night sky. Now, who knew what was star and what was rocket poised for destruction.

One star shone brighter than all the others tonight. *Three* thousand years on, was it the Christmas star? Did it promise hope?

How much more had she forgotten, besides the last lines of a song?

The Prophet

The prophet looked out across the valley toward the hill of Bethlehem. It was strange to think it was called the city of David—such a small insignificant place, lost in the middle of nowhere. "Bethlehem of Judah," he thought and wondered where he'd heard the phrase before. Of course, it *was* Bethlehem of Judah—David was the king of Judah's line. But it was such a grand name for a nothing town.

Then he began to dream.

There were people, so many people, on the road to Bethlehem. All were heading for the tiny town, on donkeys, on foot, pulling carts. There seemed so countless he couldn't imagine how they'd fit inside the city walls, but still they arrived. Among the crowd he saw a small family, a husband with his wife sitting on a donkey. He wasn't sure how he knew from this distance, but the woman seemed pregnant. He found himself feeling sorry for her—to make such a journey so late in her pregnancy.

As he watched the man and his wife, he found himself drawn to the crowds, toward the city. It was noisy in the valley and cramped. He felt almost afraid to be crowded together with so many. What would it be like when the city walls closed in around him?

Soon he was following close behind the young couple with the donkey. Now it was clear that the woman was near her time. Her husband talked to her, whispering comfort, but he couldn't hear the words. He learned that the authorities had commanded this mass influx of people— Jewish? Assyrian? He wondered who was in charge. But this wasn't the vision the prophet had hoped to see. Wasn't he looking for a new leader for the people, someone who'd renew their faith, so God would drive the Assyrians out of their land? *Why the crowds? Why the road to Bethlehem? Why Bethlehem at all—the days of David the King were long gone?*

The city gates were close, and soldiers stood guard, heavy armor weighing them down, sharp swords glinting in the sun. The ragged crowd passed between them, closely watched at every step. No-one met the soldiers' eyes. All heads were bowed as if they thought they were entering the temple for prayer.

Almost without thinking, the prophet dropped his gaze too, missing his chance to confirm if the guards were Assyrian. They didn't look Assyrian though—wrong armor. Who else could they be?

The city was packed. People lay in every corner of the streets and lined the walls. Families proudly reserved their personal patches of earth, refusing to let anyone tread where they planned to lay their heads. Beggars crawled among the healthy, demanding alms. Children scrabbled for each other's food and clothing. Every building seemed to house either soldiers or overcrowded guests. Even the roofs were thronged with faces staring down, shouting, gazing at the never-ending stream of newcomers on the street.

The man and woman he'd followed stopped at the first house they passed, and the man knocked on the door. No-one answered. Someone yelled through a window upstairs and told him to go away. It might have been the owner or just a stranger who knew there was no room. It was hard to imagine where there might be room, but the wife clearly needed a place to rest.

Suddenly a woman called out from the street, cursing the young wife, questioning the parentage of her child. The wife said nothing, and her husband didn't defend her. The prophet suddenly felt as if God were insulted but couldn't think why. Strange that he should feel himself so drawn to a woman in need, a woman scorned so easily. But it seemed as if she were touched by God and immune to human taunts. All the same, she cried, as any woman might at the time of birth.

All the houses the husband tried were full. Sometimes an owner showed sympathy. Sometime he just shouted. But no-one had room. It seemed the child might be born on the street after all, and die as children often do. It was a shame. Instinctively the prophet knew God had a reason for wanting this child to live, but what could he do?

Perhaps God would grant him the vision he needed, the end of Assyrian might, if he found a way to help. So, still in his dreaming, the prophet walked ahead of the couple in search of a place for them to stay.

Near the gates of the city, a small boy held a goat by a strip of leather. The boy looked up, cupping his hand, begging for alms. But the prophet thought only, where would the goat sleep tonight?

He saw the man and woman behind, and the man came up to the boy, asking the same question he'd asked all evening. "Please, do you know a place where we can sleep tonight?"

The boy ignored the question and looked at the woman. "You havin' a baby?"

"Yes."

"Here?"

"Where else?"

The boy frowned. "My mom had a baby," he said slowly. "It died." He paused, still holding his cupped hand out hopefully. "My goat had a baby too. It's in the stable. Stables is good for babies."

The goat tugged at the woman's skirt and began to chew contentedly. When the boy pulled it away the cloth stayed in its mouth, leaving a dark sodden hole near the woman's hem. The boy tensed, ready to flee, but the woman just smiled. "D'you want to have your baby in a stable?" he asked, by way of apology—space in a stable in exchange for a hole in her skirt. "Well, do you?"

"Yes please. Will you take us there?"

***

The prophet was back outside the city walls, and it was night. The stable was cold and dark and stank of animals. The goat was there, tied to a post with the donkey at its side. Further in were cattle munching hay and lowing to each other. The man and woman were there too, and a newborn child mewled softly in the hay. For a moment the prophet remembered his task, to find a king for his people. Was this his king? But then he forgot again and only wondered if the baby was well.

A bright star suddenly turned the night sky into day. *Signs. Portents.* The prophet was afraid because he hadn't asked for this sign and couldn't read it, and because there was something bigger here than his vision required. Crowds of people began to fill the shadows by the cave. The star stood overhead, lighting their way.

Shepherds, smelling of their flocks and the green hillside grass, arrived in a crowd. Townsfolk sleepy from their beds; strangers from the city streets leaving their precious patches of earth unguarded along the road; finally even richly garmented kings came to the manger. All bowed and honored the tiny child—surely a king indeed, even if he wasn't the king the prophet had come here to seek. They came and left in an unending stream, while the prophet stood watch, waiting unseen in the shadows, not really there.

The sky was bright in the light of the star. The shadows were sharp. Voices sang, "Hosanna to the son of David," and sounded like an angel choir. Suddenly the prophet's vision was clear, and he knew why Bethlehem was special, why he was here. He entered the stable with the others and bowed, to honor his king, his Messiah.

***

The prophet shook himself awake. Across the valley the little town lay sleeping in the afternoon sun. Who could live there of any importance he wondered? Its only glory had been King David, the greatest of Israel's kings, now long dead and gone. But perhaps there would be another leader, even if not a king. Perhaps there was someone God had brought him here to find, a man who could serve until the true king appeared. The prophet foresaw the ways of the Lord and wrote them in his book, but as he thought of Israel's salvation from Assyria, other images came to mind. Salvation for all, shepherd and king, stranger and friend, and angels singing without end.

"And you O Bethlehem, Ephratha, least of the tribes of Judah, from you shall come for me the one who is to be ruler of Israel, whose reign is from of old, from ancient days." (Micah 5:2)

It was strange, but even as he wrote the words, the vision changed. Blue sky turned black, and a dark cross hung against the clouds, a young man dying. He heard the words of David's psalm: "My God, My God, why have you forsaken me?" But that was another prophecy for another prophet to tell. Micah had written what God commanded, and now his work was done.

Old Man

"A long time ago I was a beggar in Bethlehem," the old man said. "Do you know Bethlehem? Crazy dump. The Romans had a census there, and it nearly drove everyone mad when all these old Davidians started arriving, claiming the right to stay. Crazy dump."

The boy looked up from his game on the paving stones. "No, I don't know Bethlehem," he said. "I live here, in Jerusalem."

"Well, you should know Bethlehem," said the old man. "Don't you read your prophecies?"

"Not if I can help it," said the boy. He threw a bundle of twigs to the ground, trying to make a picture from their shapes when they landed, but there was nothing there. He'd never earn his way as a grown-up beggar if he couldn't learn at least one trick.

"How do you pretend to be lame?" he asked the old man. He'd asked the same question a million times, and the answer was always the same.

"Me, pretend?"

"Yes you."

"Find out for yourself." Though the man's legs truly did look broken.

They sat in silence for a while. Most people were indoors eating their Passover meal, so the streets were clear, just the occasional marching clang of soldiers at play. The boy had hoped the strange new prophet, who borrowed his uncle's donkey, might have invited him in, but no-one seemed to have seen the man since the start of the week. The boy hadn't seen his uncle either, which was why he sat outdoors now with the beggar, instead of eating herbs and lamb with his uncle's friends.

The boy's uncle was what city folk called a "wild man." He lived in the hills and tried to drive out the Roman chariots with sticks and stones. But every Passover, someone would invite him to Jerusalem. The boy would tag along, just for a meal, though he and his uncle didn't like each other very much. The boy's uncle thought even tax-collecting was better than begging, which was why his uncle and his father stopped talking to each other.

"So what happened in Bethlehem?" the boy asked, when he got bored with his sticks.

"Well," said the beggar. "It was during that census thing, way back. There was this big fuss about a star. Folks had all sorts of stories about it, how it meant the Messiah was born, or Rome had fallen, or some such..."

"And had it?"

"Come off it, kid. Rome never falls."

Just then, some soldiers rushed out of Pilate's palace and along the street. They were armed and looked to be in a terrible hurry to arrest someone. Joshua thought he recognized the man leading them, but he wasn't sure. Perhaps he'd begged some money off him sometime.

"Carry on," he said, when the soldiers had passed. "You were saying about the star."

"Yes," said the beggar. "It was really bright. Almost like day."

Joshua looked around. The night was passing fast, but day was still a long way off, and he'd need to be well rested and awake. There would be lots of people around tomorrow, and maybe he'd beg enough money from them to buy good food. It didn't seem fair that he should go hungry while everyone else was feasting.

"Like day it was, and everyone was racing around this way and that, no-one taking any notice at all of an old beggar like me. And I couldn't even ply my trade properly because everyone else was begging.

"And there was this story they were telling, about how a woman had been turned away from the inn when she was going to have a baby, and the family house had no room, and someone rented her a stable to have the child in. They were saying the child might be the Messiah, 'cause the star came out when it was born, and everyone was trying to find out where the stable was, so they could see."

"Why?" asked Joshua.

"'Cause the Messiah's meant to be the redeemer of Israel and drive out the Romans I suppose. No-one was very keen on Romans at the census."

"Did they find him?"

"Yeah, they found the baby. So did I. Just a mutt, like any other kid if you ask me. All screams and no teeth."

He stopped. The soldiers were coming back, and there was a group of Jewish dignitaries behind them. The priests always got annoyed when they found beggars "spying" on them, so Joshua slipped away from the old man and hid behind a wall.

"Just get through the trial," one of them was saying, "and we might have him crucified tomorrow."

"Sounds good. We need to nip this thing in the bud."

"Terrorists…"

Joshua recognized the prisoner! It was the prophet he'd seen earlier, and suddenly he was quite glad he'd not shared Passover with him. A crucifixion would be good for business, but he didn't want to be on the business end of one!

The old man stayed out on the road. He really was lame, and he couldn't run. "Alms for a beggar," he called as the group marched past. "Alms for a beggar, Son of David."

The prophet turned to look at him and seemed to smile. Then they were gone.

The old man looked sad when the boy came back, but he hid his eyes behind his sleeve and said nothing.

"So he wasn't the Messiah then?" the boy asked.

"Who?"

"The baby. In Bethlehem."

"Oh yes, he was."

Joshua jumped back and banged his hand on the wall. Could the old man really be telling him that the man who would drive out the Romans had been born in a Bethlehem stable? But how? The Romans were still here.

"So where is he now?" he asked angrily. "Why doesn't he do something?"

"He's here," said the beggar, hiding his eyes again, as if he were trying not to cry. "That was him, just then. He's the prisoner."

The old man stood up and began to walk away. At first his steps were unsteady on his lame leg, but then he found his feet and stood tall and proud as any citizen. The boy stared—he'd never seen the beggar walk before; he'd almost—or nearly almost—believed he really was lame. Then he thought how his uncle Barabbas would laugh, when he told him what they'd been talking about.

Where was Uncle Barabbas anyway?

Home for Christmas

He was too young to die. Everyone agreed on that. He was sixteen and should have had his whole life before him, but instead he lay in a hospital bed, watching the doctors' grim faces and forced smiles. In winter they'd thought he'd pulled a muscle in his shoulder. In spring they'd started tests. And in summer he was in and out of the hospital, each time weaker and more afraid. The year was passing and with it his life, like raindrops vanishing in a pool.

At the foot of his bed his sister played with her dolls. The hospital smells, washed walls and iron bedstead meant nothing to her, and she ignored them. John envied her.

"The leaves are lovely this year," his mother said. It was fall.

"Yes, it's a marvelous display," said his father. "That red tree in the yard that you like so much…"

"I wish you could see it."

"It's beautiful."

His gaze wandered. He knew he should look at them and be attentive. He really ought to ignore the restless way their hands twined as they spoke. But his eyes drifted to the small square window, high-set in the wall. The sky was leaden gray, like hospital paint. At night it went black. They told him there was still a world outside with trees and leaves. Perhaps it was raining.

"What do you want for Christmas this year?"

"Autumn leaves…"

He turned back to face them. He'd spoken without thinking, and now he smiled. It must have come out right because his mother smiled back—he'd been afraid his face muscles would betray him with a grimace.

"I'm sorry, Mom," he said. "It's just I really do wish I could see them."

"Don't worry, John," she answered, taking his hand. "You'll see them next year."

***

When they got home, Kathy raced into the yard and started searching through the leaves on the ground. She made a bouquet of reds and browns and carried them up to her room. She had a vase on her windowsill which she filled with water to feed them. Then she set them in the sun.

As the week passed, Kathy's leaves wilted and grew damp. Her mother threw them out while she was tidying up. So Kathy tried again.

This time Kathy chose only the flattest, driest leaves and kept them with no water so they wouldn't get soggy. But they shrank and became sharp and brittle. They looked so ugly she threw them out herself.

"Mom," she asked in the kitchen one day. "Can you keep leaves?"

"What do you mean?"

Kathy kicked a crumb on the floor. "Well... keep them so they'll still be there in winter..."

Her mother smiled, always glad when Kathy found a new interest to amuse her. "Why yes," answered. "You have to press them flat under some heavy books, then they dry all clean and bright, and you can keep them forever. I'll even get you a scrapbook to keep them in."

"No," Kathy protested. "I don't want to keep them like that. Just keep them."

Her mother knew better than to ask what the difference was.

Autumn was passing, and most of the leaves were damp and rain-soaked now. But Kathy found one, big and red, which she could save. She hid it under her dad's encyclopedia on the bookshelf in her room. Then

45

she got her crayons out to write a note which she place on top. "Plees do not mov."

***

The priest came in early November. He wore a black coat and old-fashioned hat, both glistening with rain. And he carried a stick. He was old and placed the stick firmly in front of himself each step that he took, thumping and shuffling his way down the aisle in the hospital ward. Everyone's eyes turned to watch him pass, and he glowed in their respect. Everyone's eyes except John's.

When the priest sat loudly on the chair by John's bed, a smell of dampness drifted from his clothing. John turned. "Hello, Father," he said.

"Hello, John."

Silence cloaked them for a while, and John fidgeted under the priest's gaze. Eventually he spoke. "Are you going to tell me about dying, Father?"

"You know, then?"

"Did you think I didn't?"

The priest looked thoughtful, not answering for a moment. Then he asked, ponderously, "How do feel about it, John?"

John stared. "Come off it! How am I meant to feel?" Then, more passively, "How would you feel?"

"About dying?"

John nodded.

"I'm not sure really. It's like going home, but I'm not ready yet. I will be when it comes." He looked sadly at John, then added, more decisively, "I know where I've been and where I'm going. It's just going home."

John looked away. "Home is Mom 'n Dad 'n Kathy," he protested. When the priest nodded, he added, "So...?"

"Home is your Father in heaven too. And your parents and Kathy meeting you there when they die."

"It's not them that's..."

Softly, "I know."

They paused, watching each other in silence. Then John asked cautiously, "You know a lot about heaven then?"

The priest nodded.

"And it helps?"

"It always helps to know something about where you're going."

They both smiled, friends for a moment. "So how can I find out," said John, "if it'll be so good for me?"

The priest fumbled in the folds of his coat, and John's gaze drifted to the window and its small square of sky. Then he felt something heavy land on his lap and looked down. The priest had placed a Bible there, black-bound to match his clothing and lined in gold. It was open, and John's name was written inside the cover.

"I suggest you start with the gospels," said the priest. He seemed about to leave—a short visit. But he added, "You'll find a young man there who you'll see a lot of in heaven." Then he pushed back his chair. It scraped on the linoleum floor. When he put on his hat, a drip landed on his nose.

John exploded, "Jesus!" not sure if he was swearing or stating the obvious, and not sure he cared. Then he repeated quietly, "Jesus." This time it was a prayer.

***

"Mom, what happens when you die?" Kathy asked.

"Why?" Her mother's gaze passed several feet above her head.

"I just wondered."

"You go home to Jesus."

"Where's that?" asked Kathy. "Is it in church?"

"In heaven."

47

"Does everyone go there?"

"Everyone who's good. Everyone that we pray for... Everyone who believes that Jesus..."

Kathy frowned and looked down at the floor. "Will I go there?" she asked.

"I expect so."

"And John?"

"One day."

She pondered the answers for a while. "Doesn't it get awfully crowded?" she asked, and her mother laughed.

***

They had gone to the hospital again, just the mother and father, leaving Kathy with a friend. Fall had retreated before the cold of winter, and the leaves had faded to skeletons frail as dust.

When they sat down, John spoke first, as if he'd been rehearsing what to say. "It's okay." He leaned forward earnestly. "God will look after us. It'll all be okay." He had the Bible open on his bed.

John's mother held his hand in hers, and her eyes shone. Then his father started to cry.

***

The lights were bright on the Christmas tree in the living-room window. Kathy was wrapping the first of her presents for her friends. "Will John be home for Christmas?" she asked.

Her mother answered, "Yes, I'm sure he will."

***

"Please God, I know you answer prayers. And you promised whatever we ask in your name we'll receive..."

***

"Please Santa, I'd like..."

***

He died.

***

Christmases are rarely white, and this year was no exception. It was raining, and the cars still had their headlights on when the family went to church in the morning. The bells rang brightly, but their sound faded into mist as it left the bell-tower. And the warm light shining through the stained glass windows was swallowed, cold and gray, in the morning air.

After the service, Kathy slipped away from her parents to join the crowds thronging the stable scene. A plastic baby lay in last year's straw. She knelt at the rail and waited till no-one was looking, then she reached into her bag for a large red leaf she'd hidden there. Stretching her arm between the altar rails, she could just touch the baby's hand. Its fingers were cupped, making a perfect place to hold the leaf securely. She watched to make sure it wouldn't fall. Then she prayed silently, "It's for John."

Outside, the rain had stopped, and the sun broke through.

>>>>>>><<<<<<<

Sheila Deeth is the author of the Five Minute Bible Story Series, the Mathemafiction novels, Tails of Mystery, Inspired by Faith and Science picture and gift books, and many short stories and poems, including some in the Writers' Mill Journals. She's working on a middle-grade fantasy series, and in her spare time, she leads a local writing group called The Writers' Mill.

>>>>>>><<<<<<<